For Luz Quintana, my eighth-grade Spanish teacher

–TK

To my family and friends, who make every day as fun
and colorful as a parade

–MO

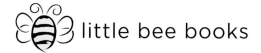 little bee books

251 Park Avenue South, New York, NY 10010
Text copyright © 2019 by Tracey Kyle | Illustrations copyright © 2019 by Mirelle Ortega | All rights reserved, including the right of
reproduction in whole or in part in any form.
Manufactured in China TPL 0819
First Edition
2 4 6 8 10 9 7 5 3 1
Library of Congress Cataloging-in-Publication Data
Names: Kyle, Tracey, author. | Ortega, Mirelle, illustrator. | Title: Pepe and the parade: a celebration of Hispanic heritage /
written by Tracey Kyle; illustrated by Mirelle Ortega.
Description: First edition. | New York, New York: Little Bee, [2019]
Summary: Pepe, who is Mexican American, enjoys participating in a festival celebrating his heritage and that of his family and
friends, who are from Chile, Ecuador, Peru, and many other countries. Includes author's note about Hispanic American History
month and the difference between the terms Hispanic and Latino. | Identifiers: LCCN 2019002527 | Subjects: CYAC: Stories in
rhyme. | Hispanic Americans—Fiction. | Latin Americans—Fiction. | Festivals—Fiction. | Classification: LCC PZ8.3.K984 Pep 2019
DDC [E]—dc23 | LC record available at https://lccn.loc.gov/2019002527
ISBN 978-1-4998-0666-3
littlebeebooks.com

PEPE AND THE PARADE

A CELEBRATION OF HISPANIC HERITAGE

Words by Tracey Kyle

Pictures by Mirelle Ortega

little bee books

Pepe wakes up early. There's a festival today!
He's going to the city with his family. *¡OLE!*

Amigos and *familia* will attend a celebration,
honoring Hispanic people all across the nation.

Pepe cannot wait to see his friends and eat *paletas*,
and hear the *mariachis* play *guitarras* and *trompetas*.

Mami makes a special breakfast filled with love and care.
The smell of *chilaquiles* and *frijoles* warms the air.

Abuelo talks of heritage, traditions, and *países*,
and says it is a festival to showcase their *raíces*.

"Today is special, Pepe, for the history and pride of millions of Hispanics who are living by our side."

Pepe makes some little flags and wants to color more.
But Mami interrupts him. "Let's get ready, *por favor!*"

Pepe loves his jersey made of radiant *colores*.
Mami is enchanting in her *falda* lined with *flores*.

Abuelo has a thing for hats and wears a wide *sombrero*.
Papi looks so dashing. Mami cries, "*¡Mi caballero!*"

The city pounds with energy and Pepe feels the pride,

remembering Abuelo's words: *Hispanics by our side.*

Pepe spots some friends from school, who are Hispanic, too.
Ana is from Ecuador and Lalo's from Perú.

Dylan is Dominican.
Andrés es panameño.

Carla is Colombian.
Tomás es hondureño.

Juan is Nicaraguan.

Teresita es chilena.

Sara is both Puerto Rican and *salvadoreña.*

Max is Guatemalan.

Santiago es cubano.

Pepe wants to join his friends and thinks, *¡Soy mexicano!*

Abuelo waves him over. "It's our turn to walk now! *¡Vamos!*"
Pepe hugs his papi, saying, "*¡Todos celebramos!*"

Abuelo shakes *maracas*. People love the *chak-chak* sound.
Pepe holds his little flags and waves them all around.

Mambo, salsa, rock, bachata, cumbia, reggaeton!

Pepe hears the mariachis start a canción.

The rhythm of the Latin music floats on down the street.

Pepe and his friends are dancing, bouncing to the beat.

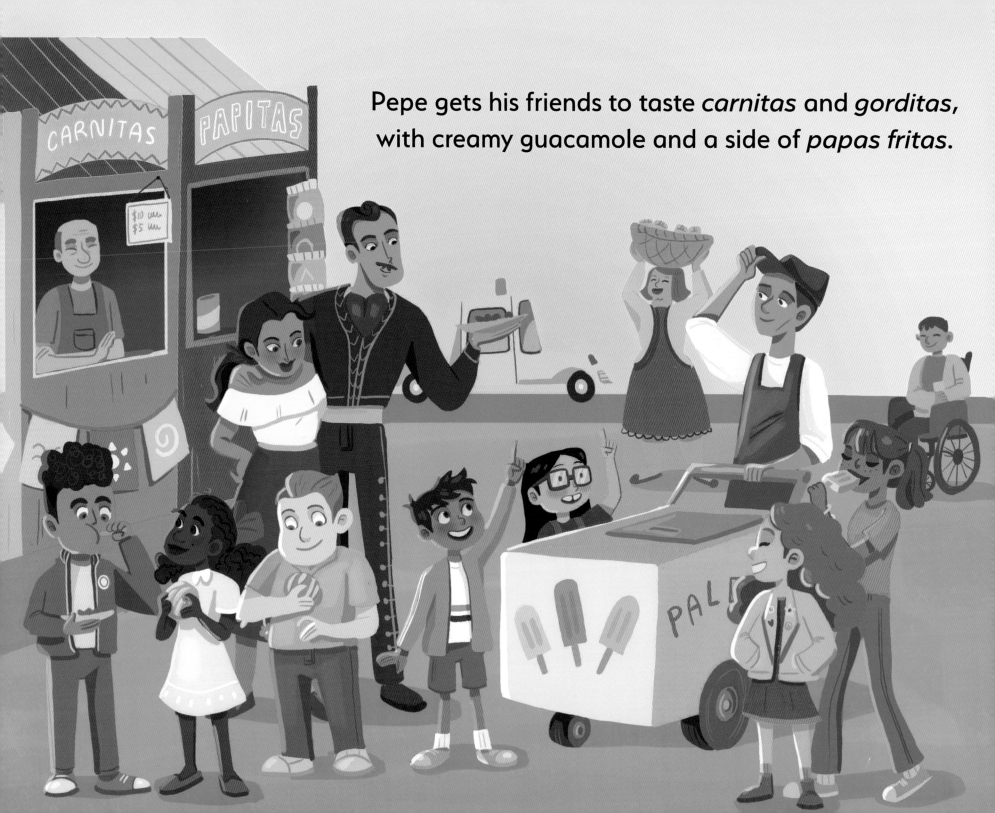

Pepe gets his friends to taste *carnitas* and *gorditas*, with creamy guacamole and a side of *papas fritas*.

"Abuelo! Take a picture!" Pepe jumps into the pile of laughing, happy, noisy kids. Abuelo chuckles, "SMILE!"

That night, when Pepe heads to bed, he feels very proud.
He knows the day was special. He could sense it in the crowd.

He falls asleep so grateful for the fun he had today,
and knows that next year's festival is just twelve months away.

AUTHOR'S NOTE

The period of time from September 15 until October 15 is known as National Hispanic Heritage Month. The United States recognizes the contributions, cultures, achievements, and history of Latino and Hispanic citizens whose ancestors come from Spain, Mexico, Central and South America, and the Caribbean. Why September 15? On that day in 1821, Guatemala, Costa Rica, Nicaragua, El Salvador, and Honduras declared their independence from Spain. Mexico declared their independence on September 16, 1810, and Chile followed on September 18, 1810. Across the United States, many cities host parades, festivals, and cultural activities commemorating these dates and celebrating the rich history of these countries.

While the terms *Hispanic* and *Latino* tend to be used interchangeably, and both include people of Latin American descent living in the United States, there are important differences. *Hispanic* refers to someone who is from a Spanish-speaking country, so it refers to language. *Latino* refers to someone from Latin America, so it refers to geography. Brazil is located in Latin America, but the primary language is Portuguese. So, Brazilians are *Latino*, but not *Hispanic*. On the other hand, Spain is a Spanish-speaking country, but it's located in Europe, not Latin America. Spaniards are *Hispanic*, but not *Latino*. Mexico is both in Latin America and is a Spanish-speaking country, so Mexicans are both *Hispanic* and *Latino*.

As a middle-school teacher, I teach a class called Spanish for Fluent Speakers. Some of my students came to the United States as small children, but most were born here. The majority of my students are of Salvadoran, Bolivian, Ecuadoran, Honduran, and Peruvian descent. These teens speak Spanish at home. In my class, we celebrate their Hispanic/Latino pride with lessons on the history, geography, art, literature, culture, and people of the Spanish-speaking world.

WEBSITES TO VISIT

- Hispanic Heritage Month: hispanicheritagemonth.org
- National Education Association: nea.org/tools/lessons/hispanic-heritage-month.html
- PBS: pbskids.org/mayaandmiguel/english/stunts/hhm/
- Scholastic: teacher.scholastic.com/scholasticnews/indepth/hispanic__heritage/

GLOSSARY (IN ORDER OF APPEARANCE)

Spanish Word	Pronunciation	English Meaning
olé	oh-LEH	hooray
(los) amigos	ah-MEE-gohs	friends
(la) familia	fah-MEE-lyah	family
(las) paletas	pah-LEH-tahs	ice pops
(los) mariachis	mah-ree-AH-chees	a small, strolling Mexican band consisting of trumpeters, guitarists, and violinists
(las) guitarras	guee-TAH-rrahs	guitars
(las) trompetas	trohm-PEH-tahs	trumpets
(los) chilaquiles	chee-lah-KEE-lehs	a traditional Mexican breakfast dish made with eggs, salsa, cheese, and tortilla
(los) frijoles	free-HOH-lehs	beans
(el) abuelo	ah-BWEH-loh	grandpa
(los) países	pie-EE-sehs	countries
(las) raíces	rye-EE-sehs	roots
por favor	POOR fah-VOOR	please
(los) colores	koh-LOH-rehs	colors
(la) falda	FAHL-dah	skirt
(las) flores	FLOH-rehs	flowers
(el) sombrero	sohm-BREH-roh	hat
mi caballero	mee kah-bah-YEH-roh	my gentleman
es panameño	EHS pah-nah-MEH-nyo	he is Panamanian
es hondureño	EHS ohn-doo-REH-nyo	he is Honduran
es chilena	EHS chee-LEH-nah	she is Chilean
salvadoreña	sahl-ba-doh-REH-nya	she is Salvadoran
es cubano	EHS koo-BAH-noh	he is Cuban
soy mexicano	SOH meh-hee-KAH-noh	I am Mexican
vamos	bah-mohs	let's go
todos celebramos	TOH-dohs seh-leh-BRAH-mohs	we're all celebrating
(las) maracas	mah-RAH-kahs	a musical instrument with a handle and a round, hollow top that is filled with beads and is shaken to make noise–prominently featured in salsa music of the Caribbean
mambo	MAHM-boh	music that developed in Cuba using saxophones, trumpets, and drums
salsa	SAHL-sah	music of Latin American origin with elements of rock, jazz, and the blues
bachata	bah-CHAH-tah	music and dance from the Dominican Republic using guitars and percussion
cumbia	KOOM-bya	music that originated in Colombia using drums, maracas, and wind instruments
reggaeton	reh-geh-TOHN	music that originated in Puerto Rico that combines rap and Caribbean rhythms
(la) canción	kahn-see-OHN	song
(las) carnitas	kar-NEE-tahs	meaning "little meats," these are pork tortillas originating in Mexico
(las) gorditas	gohr-DEE-tahs	thick tortillas stuffed with cheese
(las) papas fritas	PAH-pahs FREE-tahs	French fries